D0118908

Originally published as *Herfst met Fien en Milo* in Belgium and Holland by Clavis Uitgeverij, Hasselt–Amsterdam, 2018
English translation from the Dutch by Clavis Publishing Inc., New York

Visit us on the Web at www.clavis-publishing.com.

Fall with Lily and Milo written and illustrated by Pauline Oud

ISBN 978-1-60537-459-8

This book was printed in July 2019 at Wai Man Book Binding (China) Ltd.
Flat A, 9/F., Phase 1, Kwun Tong Industrial Centre, 472-484 Kwun Tong Road, Kwun Tong, Kowloon, H.K.

First Edition
10 9 8 7 6 5 4 3 2 1

Fall with
Lily and Milo

Pauline Oud

NEW YORK

Fall is here!
Lily and Milo are going exploring in the woods.

What will they take to carry everything they find?
Milo's little cart, a wicker basket, or a suitcase?
What does Lily choose? What does Milo choose?

Lily chooses the wicker basket and Milo takes his cart.
Milo looks through the window outside.
It has started to rain!

What should Lily and Milo wear?
A raincoat, or a bathing suit?
Rubber boots or flip-flops?

Lily and Milo wear their raincoats and boots.
That's good, because now it's raining hard.

The wind is blowing the leaves from the trees.
Look, one tree is almost completely bare.

The rain has stopped. The sun is shining!
"Hey, what's that?" Milo asks.
He points to the fence.

“That is a spider web,” says Lily.
But where is the little spider?

Lily and Milo find
some fruit trees.

Milo wants to pick up some apples.
"This is a funny apple," says Milo.
"That's not an apple," Lily laughs.
"That's a pear!"

What is crawling between the apples and pears?
A little hedgehog! He lives in a pile of leaves.
And the earthworm lives under the ground.

Lily finds a snail.
"Look, he has eyes on little stalks," says Lily.
And do you know where the snail lives?
In the little house on his back!

Hoo! Hoo! "Do you hear that?"
Lily asks softly.
"There is an owl!"

"And there is a squirrel!"
Milo points.
"And there is another one!"
Hop, hop. The squirrels jump
from branch to branch.

"Look, Milo! Acorns and pinecones!" Lily cheers.
She puts some in her basket.
Milo finds a long stick.
He looks for acorns and pinecones, too.
Will you help him?

Lily sees red mushrooms
with white spots.
"They are so pretty!
Look, Milo!"

But there are more mushrooms in the woods.
"We can't pick mushrooms," says Lily.
"They have to stay in the woods."

Lily and Milo can bring some leaves home.
Lily chooses three beautiful leaves.
Milo can't choose. All the fall leaves
are beautiful!
Which leaves would you choose?

Back home, Lily puts the nuts, leaves, and pinecones in a dish.
She puts her fruit in a bowl.
"Milo, will you put your things on the table too?" asks Lily. "Milo?"
Hey, where is Milo?

"Oh, there you are!" says Lily.
"I brought all the leaves!" Milo calls cheerfully.
"And my new friends from the forest.
Now it feels a little like fall inside, too!"